Emmy
the Exaggerating Elephant
Fenton
the Fearful Frog
Gertie
the Grungy Goat
Herbie
the Happy Hamster
Ivy
the Impatient Iguana
Ollie
the Obedient Ostrich
Perry
the Polite Porcupine
Queenie
the Quiet Quail
Rupert
the Resourceful Rhinoceros
Wendy
the Wise Woodchuck
Xavier
the X-ploring Xenops
Yori
the Yucky Yak
Ziggy
the Zippy Zebra
P9-DUJ-178

NOTE TO PARENTS

Ivy Can't Wait
A story about patience

In this story, Ivy the Impatient Iguana discovers that things that take time are worth waiting for. Because of her impatience and need for immediate gratification, Ivy has several mishaps and ends up feeling miserable. With the help of Ollie the Obedient Ostrich and her other AlphaPet friends, Ivy learns the benefit of being patient, and gets a welcome reward at the end.

In addition to enjoying this humorous story with your child, you can use it to teach a gentle lesson about the important value of patience and the benefits of thinking ahead.

You can also use this story to introduce the letter **I**. As you read about Ivy the Impatient Iguana, ask your child to listen for all the **I** words and point to the objects that begin with **I**. When you've finished reading the story, your child will enjoy doing the activity at the end of the book.

The AlphaPets™ characters were conceived and created by Ruth Lerner Perle.
Characters interpreted and designed by Deborah Colvin Borgo.
Cover/book design and production by Norton & Company.
Logo design by Deborah Colvin Borgo and Nancy S. Norton.
Printed and Manufactured in the United States of America

Ivy Can't Wait

RUTH LERNER PERLE
Illustrated by Richard Max Kolding

Grolier Enterprises, Inc., Danbury, Connecticut

One sunny spring day, some of the AlphaPets received a letter written in brightly colored ink. It was an invitation from Ollie the Obedient Ostrich.

My Dear Friend,
The weather is getting warmer, the days are getting longer, and summer will be here soon. The trees are blooming in the orchard, and the strawberries are ripe for picking.
Please come to visit me in the country. We'll have lots of fun, and we can enjoy some yummy strawberry shortcake and iced tea in the gazebo.

Your friend,
Ollie

"If you'd like to visit Ollie today, I'll be glad to drive you all," said Perry the Polite Porcupine.

"Oh, that would be so nice," said Lizzy the Lazy Lamb. "The fresh country air is so relaxing."

"Well, well, well, well," said Vinnie the Vocal Vulture. "What an absolutely superb idea. I would dearly love to be in the country again."

"Ooh, I can't wait to get to Ollie's," said Ivy the Impatient Iguana. "I can almost taste that strawberry shortcake! *Mmm mmm!* It's my very favorite treat. Let's leave *now*!"

"We can't leave just yet," said Perry. "First, I have to fill the car with gas."

"But I want to go *now*!" cried Ivy.

"Please be patient, Ivy," Perry said. "If we don't plan ahead, we'll run out of gas, and then we'll *never* get to Ollie's. I'll pick you all up in a half-hour."

Perry got into his car and drove off to the gas station.

When Perry came back, Ivy was the first to jump in the car.

"Hurry up, everybody," she shouted. "The sooner we leave, the sooner we'll have that strawberry shortcake."

Perry gave his windshield a last polish, and got in behind the driver's wheel. Lizzy and Vinnie sat in the back seat.

Everybody buckled their seat belts, and they drove off.

After just a few minutes, Lizzy was fast asleep, and Vinnie was busy looking at the road map and reading all the road signs.

"Are we there yet?" Ivy asked.

"Oh, no, no, no. We have quite a long way to go," said Vinnie. "Be patient, Ivy. It's a perfect day. A lovely day for a nice, slow, ride in the country."

SLOW

"Slow, shmow!" said Ivy. "*Faster*, Perry! I want to get to that shortcake as fast as possible."

"I can't go faster than the speed limit," said Perry. "Please try to relax and enjoy the ride, Ivy."

But Ivy couldn't relax. Every few minutes, she jumped up and wanted to know if they were at Ollie's yet.

When the AlphaPets finally arrived at Ollie's Orchard, Ollie came out to greet them.

"Welcome, welcome!" said Ollie. "Isn't this a lovely, lazy, day!"

Ivy jumped out of the car. "Hi, Ollie," she cried. "Can we have that strawberry shortcake now?"

"Oh, it's too early for cake and tea," Ollie answered.

"Let's all go down to the lake, then," suggested Perry.

"The water is still too cold for swimming," said Ollie. "It won't be warm enough for at least a month. But we can play ball down there if you like."

While the others went to get the ball, Ivy ran down to the lake. She took off her shoes and socks and stepped into the water.

"*YOW!!!*" she yelled.

The water was icy and Ivy's feet were *freezing*. "Maybe I should have listened to Ollie," she thought. Ivy dashed out of the water and put on her shoes and socks.

Then she ran to where the others were playing catch. Vinnie was throwing the ball, and the AlphaPets took turns catching it.

“Get in line, Ivy,” called Ollie. “It will be your turn soon. Perry is next.”

But Ivy couldn’t wait. When Vinnie threw the ball, she jumped up to get it before Perry could.

“Hey! That’s not fair,” said Lizzy.

In her rush for the ball, Ivy didn’t look where she was going.

“Look out!” called Ollie.

Thwack! Ivy ran into a tree and bumped her head.

The AlphaPets ran over to Ivy. They put ice cubes on Ivy’s bump and a Band-Aid on her cut.

When Ivy was feeling better, everyone went back to the house.

"Can we have strawberry shortcake now?" asked Ivy.

"I guess we can get started," Ollie said. "I'll put the cakes in the oven and whip the cream. You all can go out to the berry patch and pick some strawberries."

Ollie gave everyone a small basket. "If you each fill your basket, you'll have just enough berries for your very own cake."

When the AlphaPets got to the berry patch, Lizzy sat down to rest. "The sun and fresh air make me *soooo* lazy," she said with a great big yawn.

"I must say, it is truly beautiful here! Yes it is, indeed!" said Vinnie. "Just look at the flowers, and all these busy, busy, insects. I could watch them for hours and hours. The ants are working in their ant hills and the bees are all busy collecting pollen."

"I wish you'd all get busy picking these berries!" called Ivy. So everyone started to fill their baskets.

When their baskets were filled, the AlphaPets started back to the house.

On the way, Ivy looked at her basket of berries. “These strawberries sure look and smell delicious,” she thought. “I think I’ll eat a few now.”

Ivy reached into the basket, took one big berry, and popped it into her mouth.

"*Yum!*" Ivy said, smacking her lips.

Then she took another berry.

And another. And another.

By the time she came back to the house, Ivy's basket was empty.

Ollie was waiting in the kitchen when the AlphaPets returned.

"Mmm! those cakes smell so delicious!" said Ivy. "But I ate all my berries. Now I won't have any for my cake."

"Oh, dear," Ollie said. "Well, you can still have the shortcake and cream."

"Oh, good!" said Ivy. "Are they ready now?"

Ollie looked at the timer. "The cakes haven't finished baking yet, but they will be ready soon," he said.

Ollie went outside to the gazebo to set the table.

"Those cakes smell ready to me," thought Ivy. "I'll just take mine out now. I can't wait."

Ivy opened the oven, and picked up one of the cakes. But it was so hot and soft that it broke into pieces.

Ivy looked at her crumbled cake. "I guess I should have waited until the cake finished baking. Maybe some whipped cream will fix it," she said. Ivy plopped a dollop of cream on her cake. But the cake was still warm and the cream started to melt and run down the sides.

Ivy's eyes filled with tears. "Oh dear, now my cake is ruined," she cried.

Soon the rest of the cakes were baked and cooled. Ivy watched as the others put strawberries and whipped cream on their cakes and took them out into the ivy-covered gazebo.

When they sat down to eat, the AlphaPets saw that Ivy was feeling very sad, so they each gave her a taste of their cake.

Ivy thanked them and said, "I guess Ollie was right. I should have waited."

Ollie poured iced tea, and then Vinnie got up to make a speech. He cleared his throat and said:

"My dear, dear friends, I cannot let the day go by without saying just a few words to our dear and generous host, Ollie. Spring is a most delightful, and glorious time to see the wonders of mother nature. The birds are building their nests and sitting *patiently* on their eggs. The caterpillars weave their cocoons ever so carefully. The fruit trees bud and blossom, and the fruits grow bigger and sweeter until the time comes for them to be picked. Nature does everything in its own good time. It can't be rushed. There's a lot we can learn from good old mother nature.
Thank you, Ollie, for this wonderful, lovely day in the country."

Everyone applauded and finished eating and drinking.

Soon Perry announced that it was time to go.

When everyone was in the car and ready to leave, Ollie came running over. He gave Ivy a little package. "Here is something for you, Ivy" said Ollie. "Be patient. Don't open this until you get home. That way you'll have something to look forward to, and you'll enjoy it more."

Ivy thanked Ollie and set the package down.

As they were riding home, Ivy kept wondering what was in the package. She wanted to take a peek, but every time she started to open the package, she remembered what Ollie said about patience. After a while she even enjoyed thinking and wondering about her surprise.

When the AlphaPets arrived home, they went to Ivy's house to watch her open the package. Carefully, she untied the string and took off the wrapping paper. She opened the box.

In the box, was a beautiful strawberry shortcake, along with a note.

> Dear Ivy,
> I hope it's not too late for you to enjoy this treat.
> Remember, there's no short cut to shortcake.
> Your friend,
> Ollie

Ivy smiled and took a big bite of cake. Then she offered some to all her friends.

"This treat was certainly worth waiting for!" she said.

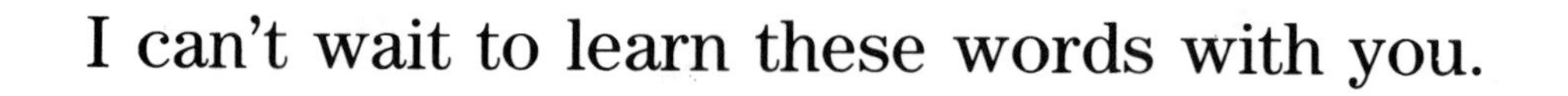
I can’t wait to learn these words with you.

iron

iris

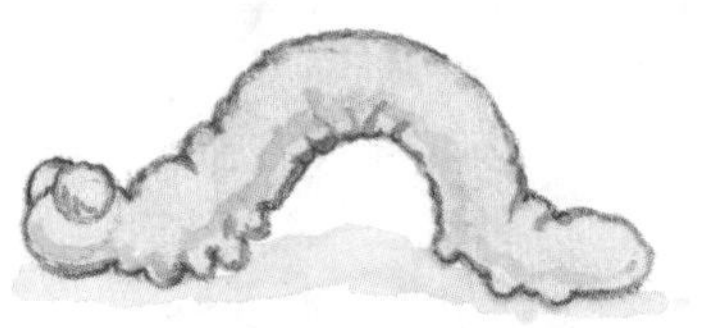

inchworm

ivy

Look back at the pictures in this book and try to find these and other things that begin with the letter I.

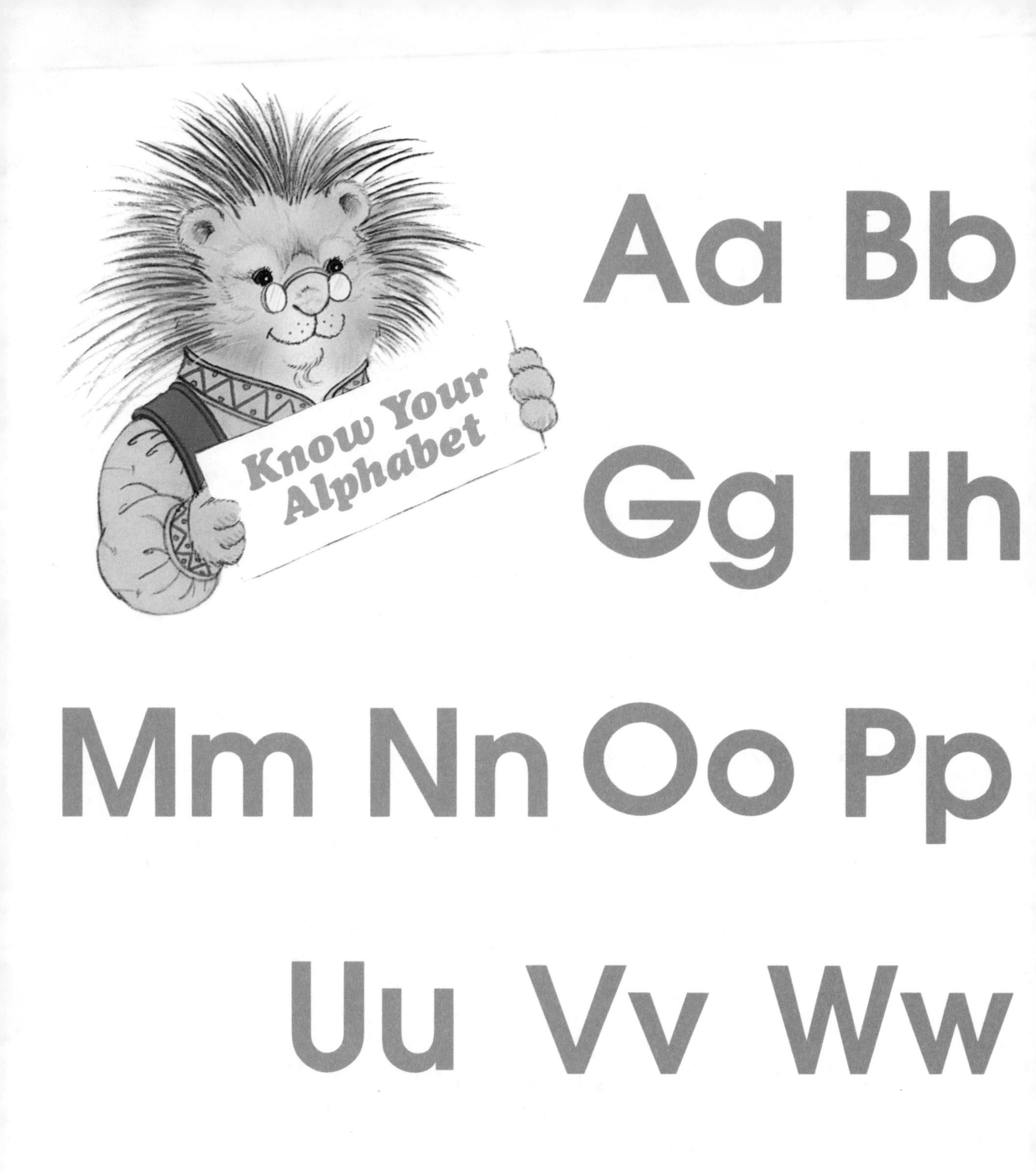
Know Your Alphabet
Aa Bb
Gg Hh
Mm Nn Oo Pp
Uu Vv Ww